SPORTY KIDS

NETBALL

COLLECT ALL THE SPORTY KIDS!

Joe is awesome at footy.
So why is handballing
so hard?

Emma is a swimming
superstar. But can she
learn to dive?

Stefan has winning
racquet skills. But will
he ever play a real
game of tennis?

Abby always wins
at soccer. So why won't
Pete join her team?

Luca never loses on the
handball court. But can
he beat the school's
Handball King?

Jessica is a basketball all-
star. So why does she need
lucky shoes?

Pete's family is crazy for
cricket. But can he take
home the Jacaranda Cup?

FELICE ARENA
ILLUSTRATED BY TOM JELLETT

SPORTY KIDS

NETBALL

PUFFIN BOOKS

PUFFIN BOOKS

UK | USA | Canada | Ireland | Australia
India | New Zealand | South Africa | China

Penguin Books is part of the Penguin Random House group of companies
whose addresses can be found at global.penguinrandomhouse.com.

Penguin
Random House
Australia

First published by Penguin Random House Australia Pty Ltd, 2016

1 3 5 7 9 10 8 6 4 2

Text copyright © Red Wolf Entertainment Pty Ltd, 2016
Illustrations copyright © Tom Jellett, 2016

Design by Tony Palmer © Penguin Random House Australia Pty Ltd
Typeset in 18pt New Century Schoolbook
Colour separation by Splitting Image Colour Studio, Clayton, Victoria
Printed and bound in Australia by Griffin Press,
an accredited ISO AS/NZS 14001
Environmental Management Systems printer.

National Library of Australia Cataloguing-in-Publication data:
Arena, Felice, author.
Netball/Felice Arena; with illustrations by Tom Jellett.

ISBN 978 0 14 330908 6

Series: Arena, Felice. Sporty kids.
Other Creators/Contributors: Jellett, Tom, illustrator.

A823.3

CHAPTER ONE

'Quick, Sofia! Get rid of the ball!' Lizzie called. 'And Jacqui, you're not allowed in the goal circle – you're Wing Defence!'

Lizzie knew everything there was to know about netball.

Her dream was to become a netball coach for the Australian Netball League. She wanted to be just like her coach, Coach Laura.

'Shush, Lizzie,' said
Jacqui as she ran past.
'Just because you're playing
Centre, doesn't mean you're
the centre of the game.'

I'm just trying to help,
thought Lizzie as she
stopped a pass from the
opposition. She threw the
ball to Ben.

An opposition player ran for the ball too, but Ben was too fast for her.

He stepped in front and caught the ball. He nearly fumbled and dropped it, but he managed to hold on.

Then he took a shot for goal and scored!

'That was fantastic, Ben!' yelled Sofia, running in to give him a high-five.

'Netball is awesome!'
yelled Oliver.

'Keep your fingers wide
apart, Ben. You'll have
better control of the ball,'
said Lizzie.

Just then the umpire
blew her whistle for
half-time.

'Keep up the good work,
everyone,' said Jacqui.

'But don't slack off,' said
Lizzie, as she and her
teammates joined their
coach on the sidelines.
'Sofia, make sure when you
pass the ball it's fast and
direct.'

Sofia and Jacqui looked
at each other and rolled
their eyes.

CHAPTER TWO

Lizzie and the team
huddled in around Coach
Laura. Lizzie couldn't wait
to hear her advice.

'Great game so far,
everyone,' Coach Laura said.

'Remember the skills we learnt in training last week. And make sure you follow through with your arm after you've thrown the ball.'

Lizzie nodded. 'Especially you, Lucy,' she said. 'And, Angus, good Goal Keepers need to stand really tall when defending.'

Angus didn't say anything but he looked cross.

'Thanks, Lizzie, that's
true, but I'm speaking now,'
said Coach Laura.

Jake, Coach Laura's son, handed out oranges he had cut for the team.

Everyone showed off their orange smiles and made each other giggle by pulling faces.

Lizzie's piece was too big to fit in her mouth. 'Next time, Jake, you should try cutting the oranges into smaller pieces,' she said.

Jake took out his orange and made a face at her.

After the break it was Lizzie's turn to sit on the bench with Coach Laura. Abby took over her position on court.

Abby was a fast runner and could throw the ball straight and hard. She always did well in Centre.

Coach Laura clapped as the ball zipped around the court.

Lizzie could see that Lucy was finding it hard to keep up.

'Hey, Lucy!' she called. 'You have to keep running!'

Coach Laura turned to Lizzie. 'I love how keen you are,' she said, 'but let's just have some fun today. Don't worry too much about how everyone is playing. That's what I'm here for, okay?'

'Okay,' said Lizzie, but
she could see that Lucy had
stopped on the court to rest.

'Lucy!' she called. 'You have
to attack and defend . . . all
the time, got it?'

CHAPTER THREE

By the end of the game, the other team had shot more goals.

'I think we need an extra training session,' said Lizzie. 'Ben, you've got to

take more chances in the
goal circle!'

'And Lucy and Jess, more defensive drill practice – that's what you need.'

But no one replied. In fact, no one said a word to Lizzie about anything.

On the ride home, Lizzie excitedly replayed the entire game to her parents.

Netball games were always the best part of her week.

But then Lizzie saw
something that made her
stop talking.

Across the road she saw
Sofia and Jacqui and the
rest of her teammates.

They were sitting outside
a cafe with frozen yoghurts.
They looked as if they were
having lots of fun.

Lizzie didn't know what to think. Did someone forget to tell me they were meeting up? she wondered.

But then she thought of
something worse!

Is it possible that they
don't want me there?

She spent the rest of the day sniffling and watching netball clips on YouTube under her bedcovers.

CHAPTER FOUR

Lizzie didn't say a word to any of her teammates all week.

At the next game she put her hand up to sit on the bench.

She sat silently next to the coach.

'You haven't said anything about the game since it started,' said Coach Laura. 'Are you okay?'

Lizzie nodded. But she *wasn't* okay.

In the second quarter, their team started to fall behind. Sofia was having a tough time against her opponent, Anthony.

He was very fast in the
centre, and Sofia couldn't
keep up.

The other team's Goal
Attack, Isabella, was really
good.

She shot goal after goal
after goal . . .

At half-time, when Lizzie's team left the court, they all looked upset, especially Jessica.

'It's all right, everyone,' Coach Laura said. 'Cheer up! You're all playing really well. I've seen some great skills out there! Jessica don't feel down – you did your best as Keeper.'

'Jacqui and Lizzie, you're my unofficial assistant coaches. You always have good advice for the team. What should we do?'

For the first time all week, Lizzie felt excited. Her favourite thing in the world was when Coach Laura called on her and Jacqui to share their ideas.

But then she started to feel nervous.

What if none of the team wanted to hear what she had to say? What if that was why they hadn't invited her after the game last week?

CHAPTER FIVE

'We're playing as well as
we always do,' said Jacqui.
'They're just faster and
taller than us.'

'What about defence?'
said Coach Laura. 'Lizzie,

What do you think?'

But Lizzie didn't know
what to say. She did have
an idea. A really good idea.
But then she remembered
Sofia rolling her eyes at the
last game.

'Um, I think it's probably best if I keep my mouth shut,' she said quietly.

'I saw you all getting frozen yogurt without me. I know you don't really like what I've got to say.'

Lizzie felt her face go red and tears began to well in her eyes – she wiped them away quickly.

Now she was feeling

embarrassed, so she turned
and walked away.

But someone was running after her. She turned around expecting it to be Coach Laura, but it was Sofia.

'Hey, Lizzie,' Sofia said.
'Wait up! You can't leave
when we need you!'
She threw Lizzie the ball.

'We're all sorry about the other day,' said Sofia. 'It's not true that no one likes what you've got to say. They do! *I* do! But sometimes it makes us feel bad.'

Lizzie nodded. 'I'm sorry too,' she said. 'I didn't mean to upset you. I just love being a coach. I'll try to say things differently next time.'

Sofia and Lizzie walked back to the team together.

'Being a coach can be hard,' Coach Laura said, and she gave Lizzie a hug as well.

'Come on, Lizzie,' said Jacqui. 'Tell us what we should do.'

'Well,' said Lizzie, 'I think there *is* a way we can block Isabella's shots.'

'Even I'm not tall enough to do that,' said Oliver.

Lizzie grinned. 'This idea might seem crazy, but I think it will work.'

'What is it?' everyone asked at the same time.

CHAPTER SIX

The teams headed back
onto the court. Oliver was
Goal Keeper and Lucy was
Goal Defence.

It didn't take long for the
other team to get the ball.

Anthony turned and
passed it towards the circle.

Lucy almost caught it,
but Isabella got there first.

Oliver was between her
and the ring, but he didn't
make himself as tall as he
could to try and block the
ball. He held his arms low
and bent his knees a little.
He looked as *small* as he
possibly could . . .

Isabella aimed at the ring
and threw the ball so it
would fly just over Oliver.

But then Oliver stretched
out to his true height and
tapped the ball!

Lucy caught it and
passed it to Sofia.

Sofia threw it safely down
the court to Abby.

They all cheered. It felt great – almost as if they had won the game!

'Lizzie,' said Coach Laura. 'I think you're going to be a great coach.'

And Lizzie couldn't wipe the smile off her face.

READ THE BOOKS AND MEET THE SPORTY KIDS...

Abby Walsh

Abby loves to win, especially at soccer. It's her favourite sport and she's the star of the team. She's got the skills to take on anyone!

Angus is fast, clever and knows everything there is to know about Aussie Rules. He's awesome in attack – the footy team's top goal-scorer.

Angus Chung

61

Ben Jakande

Ben is a fan of everything sporty. He knows all the players, all the stats and every sporting record there is. He's a walking, talking wikipedia of sport!

Emma is creative and loves acting almost as much as sport. She's a great all-rounder with an original way of looking at every sporting situation.

Emma Ashworth

62

Jacqui can tell you who to play in what position, and which tactics to use – she's the brains behind any team. Need a winning strategy? Ask Jacqui!

Jacqui Abraham

Jessica Ito

Jessica is the smallest in the class, but she's also the star of the basketball team. She won't brag about it, though – she thinks she's just very very lucky!

Joe Meyer

Joe is funny, cheeky and loves team sports. He's a terrific all-rounder and a natural at almost everything, so he's keen to give anything a try.

Lizzie is the heart of any team. She's the commentator, scorer and cheer squad, all rolled into one. No one loves sport more than Lizzie!

Lizzie Passad

Luca is super strong and super confident, like his twin sister, Sofia. He's a natural leader and the king of the handball courts at lunch.

Luca Facelli

Lucy Ko

Lucy is the fastest kid in class. She's not so keen on playing team sports – but she's super fit and the queen of the athletics track.

Oliver is bigger and stronger than anyone else in class. His favourite sport is swimming. He's not so good at losing – but that's because he usually wins!

Pete is the ultimate team player, but he also loves to win. He knows how to bring a team together to get the best out of everyone.

Sofia is lots of fun and is super competitive, like her twin brother, Luca. She's awesome at sport, especially ball sports, and she's always the first picked for any team.

Stefan is imaginative and very independent so he loves individual sports like tennis. Give him a sporting skill to learn and he's all over it!

COACH LAURA'S TIPS ON HOW TO SHOOT

Lizzie's strategy is a good one –
never let the goal shooters know
how high you can block the ball
until it's too late.

But what if *your* team is
attacking? Listen to your coach for
any extra tips and practise every
day.

If you're giving advice, like Lizzie,
here's the best way to shoot. But
remember, a good coach is kind and
focuses on the positive!

Here's how to shoot for goal:

- Stand within the shooting semicircle.
- Make sure your feet are shoulder width apart and pointing at the post.
- Straighten your arm close to your ear with the ball held in that hand – your fingers should face away from the ring. Steady the ball with your other hand.
- Aim above the ring so it falls through without touching it.

Other netball skills include chest and shoulder passes. And, remember, netball is a game for absolutely everyone!

LIZZIE'S FAVOURITE NETBALL JOKES!

Why was Cinderella's netball team
so bad?
Her coach was a pumpkin.

What's the difference between a
netball hog and time?
Time passes.

Why was the netball stadium hot
after the game?
Because all the fans had left.

What do eagles do when they coach
a netball team?
They wing it!

Knock! Knock!
Who's there?
Harry
Harry who?
Harry up, and play netball with me!

Why is a scrambled egg like a losing
netball team?
Because they both have been beaten.

Why is basketball messier
than netball?
Because basketball players dribble –
and they don't even wear bibs!

What did the netball player say
to the ball?
Catch you later!

LIZZIE'S AWESOME NETBALL FACTS!

Did you know?

- When playing netball you can only hold the ball for three seconds. If you hold it for over three seconds it is called a 'held ball' violation.
- Defenders must be at least 90 centimetres away from the player with the ball.
- Around 20 million people play netball worldwide.
- Different forms of netball include mixed netball, indoor netball and 'netta' for kids.

- In official mixed netball games there must always be one boy on the court and no more than three boys on the court at one time.
- Netball evolved from basketball in the 1890s – women couldn't play basketball in the long dresses and heavy clothes they had to wear, so they changed some of the rules and netball was born!
- In 1995 netball became a recognised Olympic sport, but it hasn't yet been played at an Olympic games.

FELICE SAYS . . .

When I first played netball I kept forgetting that I couldn't bounce the ball like I did in basketball. In fact, once, our coach pulled me off the court mid-game and handed me a handkerchief. 'Here, Felice!' she said. 'You'll need this if you're going to dribble so much!' Everyone laughed – even my own teammates!

TOM SAYS . . .

Felice has finally written about a sport I haven't tried yet! It looks terrific! I'm not sure which position would be best for me, maybe WA – I think that stands for 'Western Australia'. If Felice writes Sporty Kids: *Golf,* then that will be TWO new sports for me to try . . .